SHARE A STORY

Introduction

One of the best ways you can help
your children learn and learn to read
is to share books with them. Here's why:

• They get to know the **sounds**, **rhythms** and **words**
used in the way we write. This is different from how we
talk, so hearing stories helps children learn how to read.

• They think about the **feelings** of the characters
in the book. This helps them as they go about
their own lives with other people.

• They think about the **ideas** in the book. This helps
them to understand the world.

• Sharing books and listening to what your children
say about them shows your children that you care
about them, you care about what they think
and who they are.

Michael Rosen
Writer and Poet
Children's Laureate (2007-9)

For Neil Ellice

First published 2004 by Walker Books Ltd
87 Vauxhall Walk, London SE11 5HJ

This edition published 2011

2 4 6 8 10 9 7 5 3 1

This book has been typeset in Handwriter

Printed in China

British Library Cataloguing in Publication Data:
a catalogue record for this book is available from the British Library

ISBN 978-1-4063-3511-8

www.walker.co.uk

Dog Blue

Polly Dunbar

WALKER BOOKS
AND SUBSIDIARIES
LONDON · BOSTON · SYDNEY · AUCKLAND

Bertie loved blue.

He had a blue
jumper,

a blue dog
collar,

blue shoes,

but no blue dog.

What Bertie wanted

more than anything in the

whole wide world was a dog.

A blue dog!

So Bertie pretended
he had a blue dog.

He patted his
pretend blue dog.

He fed his pretend
blue dog.

He took his pretend
blue dog for a walk.

He threw a stick for
his pretend blue dog.

But pretend dogs don't fetch sticks.

So Bertie fetched the stick himself.

Bertie pretended
he was a dog,
a blue dog.

He scratched
like a blue dog.

He sniffed
like a blue dog.

He chased his

tail like

a blue

dog.

And Bertie yapped like a blue dog.

YAP!

A
real dog
yapped
back!

A tiny dog,

all alone
and looking for
an owner.

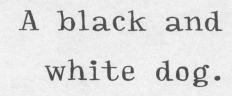
A black and white dog.

A beautiful, spotty dog.

A perfect dog.

Bertie's dog!

But hang on ...

wait a moment...

Bertie's
dog isn't
blue at
all!

Bertie thought and thought.
If this black and white,
beautiful, spotty,

perfect dog

were his dog

but not a

blue

dog ...

hen he must give the dog something blue ...

a name!

BLUE!

Bertie called his dog Blue.

What a perfect pair!

Bertie took Blue for a walk.

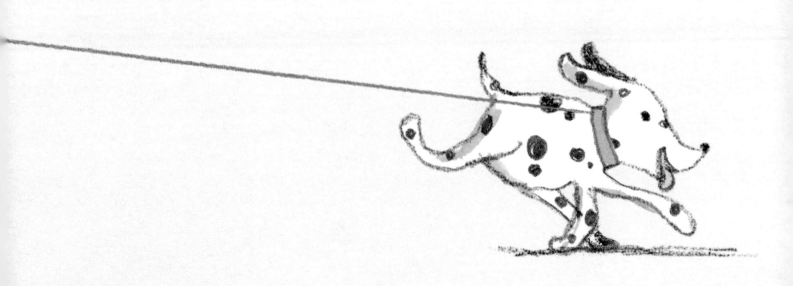

Blue took Bertie for a walk.

Bertie fed Blue.

Blue sniffed Bertie.

Bertie patted Blue.

Blue wagged his tail.

Then Blue
showed Bertie how
tail-chasing is done,
when you're a real dog
and you really
have a
tail.

So Bertie doesn't
need to pretend any more.

Blue really loves Bertie.

Bertie really loves Blue.

Especially when ...

it's Bertie's turn to fetch!

Sharing Stories

Sharing stories together is a pleasurable way to help children learn to read and enjoy books. Reading stories aloud and encouraging children to talk about the pictures and join in with parts of the story they know well are good ways to build their interest in books. They will want to share their favourite books again and again. This is an important part of becoming a successful reader.

Dog Blue is a gentle, amusing story about a little boy who desperately wants to have a dog, a blue dog, and enjoys pretending he does. Then one day, he meets a real dog and his dream comes true. There's only one problem… Here are some ways you can share this book:

• After reading the story aloud a few times and talking about it together, encourage your child to use the pictures to help them to retell the story in their own words. You can do this by beginning it yourself and then taking it in turns as you go through the book.

• In the story, Bertie pretends to own a dog and then pretends to *be* a dog. What kind of dog does your child want to be? They can draw a dog of their choice and then pretend to be the dog – scampering, chasing, tail-wagging, barking and having their tummy tickled.

• Blue was all alone when Bertie met him. Talk together about why that might have been. Children can invent and tell their own story about Blue before he met Bertie.

• Perhaps you have a family dog or know some dogs. Ask your child to tell you their favourite dog names. What do they think makes a good name?

• Think of about 6 to 10 different names and make name (or collar) tags for each one on squares of paper. Together, find names beginning with the same letter. Children can also sort them into groups of names that end with the same letter or into groups of names with one, two or three syllables. Perhaps they can try putting them in alphabetical order.

• Bertie loves blue. You could have a treasure hunt collecting together anything blue that can be moved! Or children could make a collage of a blue dog, using magazine pictures, food wrappings, fabric, paint and crayon.

SHARE A STORY
A First Reading Programme
From Pre-school to School

Beginnings – 2 years+

Look Out, Suzy Goose — Petr Horáček
Walking Through the Jungle — Julie Lacome (Introduced by Michael Rosen)
Hello, Goodbye — David Lloyd, Louise Voce (Introduced by Michael Rosen)
Ten in the Bed — Penny Dale (Introduced by Michael Rosen)
This Is the Bear — Sarah Hayes, Helen Craig (Introduced by Michael Rosen)
The Big Wide-Mouthed Frog — Ana Martín Larrañaga (Introduced by Michael Rosen)

Early Steps – 3 years+

A New House for Mouse — Petr Horáček
The Train Ride — June Crebbin, Stephen Lambert (Introduced by Michael Rosen)
The Other Day I Met a Bear — Russell Ayto (Introduced by Michael Rosen)
Old MacDonald Had a Farm — Jane Chapman (Introduced by Michael Rosen)
Beans on Toast — Paul Dowling (Introduced by Michael Rosen)
Zed's Bread — Mick Manning, Brita Granström (Introduced by Michael Rosen)

Next Steps – 4 years+

The Hairy Toe — Daniel Postgate (Introduced by Michael Rosen)
The True Story of Humpty Dumpty — Sarah Hayes, Charlotte Voake (Introduced by Michael Rosen)
Beans on Toast — Paul Dowling (Introduced by Michael Rosen)
Over in the Meadow — A Counting Rhyme — Louise Voce (Introduced by Michael Rosen)
Dog Blue — Polly Dunbar (Introduced by Michael Rosen)
Night-night, Knight And Other Poems — Michael Rosen, Sue Heap (Introduced by Michael Rosen)

Taking Off – 5 years+

"Have You Seen the Crocodile?" — Colin West (Introduced by Michael Rosen)
Handa's Surprise — Eileen Browne (Introduced by Michael Rosen)
The Ravenous Beast — Niamh Sharkey (Introduced by Michael Rosen)
One, Two, Flea! — Allan Ahlberg, Colin McNaughton (Introduced by Michael Rosen)
Dinosaurs' Day Out — Nick Sharratt (Introduced by Michael Rosen)
The Old Woman and the Red Pumpkin — Betsy Bang, Rachel Merriman (Introduced by Michael Rosen)

Sharing the best books makes the best readers

WALKER BOOKS

www.walker.co.uk